Leapfrog
Rhyme
Time

Dan's Gran's Goat

by Joan Stimson

Illustrated by Beccy Blake

W
FRANKLIN WATTS
LONDON•SYDNEY

Dan's gran had a goat called Scruff.

His beard was a mess
and his coat was rough.

7

"Scruff needs a wash," said Gran one day.

"And Dan can help when he comes to stay."

9

Dan came to stay and
he tried not to laugh,

when out of the shed
came an old tin bath.

"Help!" thought Scruff
and off Scruff ran.

So off sped Gran,
and off sped Dan!

Scruff ran to the park.

He slid down the slide.

14

"Come back Scruff!"
Dan's gran cried.

Dan cried, too.

"It's time to stop!"

But Scruff ran on
and into a shop.

Inside the shop,
Scruff toppled tins.

SOUP
on offer
THIS WEEK
ONLY

18

He scattered fruit.

He emptied bins.

He nibbled here,

he gobbled there.

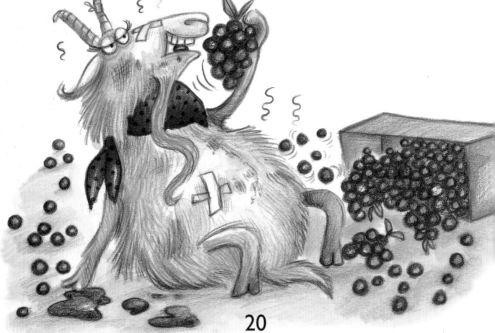

20

He scoffed a pie,

he gulped a pear.

21

Outside the shop,
Scruff burped and then
he raced on down
the road again.

BUR

23

But down the road,
old Mr Rose
had just turned on
his garden hose.

And when Dan yelled:

"Quick! Help us please!"

He gave that hose
a mighty squeeze!

27

So, in the end,
Scruff got his wash.

29

"Oh, Scruff," beamed Gran.
"You do look posh!"

Leapfrog has been specially designed to fit the requirements of the National Literacy Strategy. It offers real books for beginning readers by top authors and illustrators.

There are 55 Leapfrog stories to choose from:

The Bossy Cockerel
ISBN 0 7496 3828 1

Bill's Baggy Trousers
ISBN 0 7496 3829 X

Mr Spotty's Potty
ISBN 0 7496 3831 1

Little Joe's Big Race
ISBN 0 7496 3832 X

The Little Star
ISBN 0 7496 3833 8

The Cheeky Monkey
ISBN 0 7496 3830 3

Selfish Sophie
ISBN 0 7496 4385 4

Recycled!
ISBN 0 7496 4388 9

Felix on the Move
ISBN 0 7496 4387 0

Pippa and Poppa
ISBN 0 7496 4386 2

Jack's Party
ISBN 0 7496 4389 7

The Best Snowman
ISBN 0 7496 4390 0

Eight Enormous Elephants
ISBN 0 7496 4634 9

Mary and the Fairy
ISBN 0 7496 4633 0

The Crying Princess
ISBN 0 7496 4632 2

Jasper and Jess
ISBN 0 7496 4081 2

The Lazy Scarecrow
ISBN 0 7496 4082 0

The Naughty Puppy
ISBN 0 7496 4383 8

Freddie's Fears
ISBN 0 7496 4382 X

FAIRY TALES
Cinderella
ISBN 0 7496 4228 9

The Three Little Pigs
ISBN 0 7496 4227 0

Jack and the Beanstalk
ISBN 0 7496 4229 7

The Three Billy Goats Gruff
ISBN 0 7496 4226 2

Goldilocks and the Three Bears
ISBN 0 7496 4225 4

Little Red Riding Hood
ISBN 0 7496 4224 6

Rapunzel
ISBN 0 7496 6159 3

Snow White
ISBN 0 7496 6161 5

The Emperor's New Clothes
ISBN 0 7496 6163 1

The Pied Piper of Hamelin
ISBN 0 7496 6164 X

Hansel and Gretel
ISBN 0 7496 6162 3

The Sleeping Beauty
ISBN 0 7496 6160 7

Rumpelstiltskin
ISBN 0 7496 6165 8

The Ugly Duckling
ISBN 0 7496 6166 6

Puss in Boots
ISBN 0 7496 6167 4

The Frog Prince
ISBN 0 7496 6168 2

The Princess and the Pea
ISBN 0 7496 6169 0

Dick Whittington
ISBN 0 7496 6170 4

The Elves and the Shoemaker
ISBN 0 7496 6575 0*
ISBN 0 7496 6581 5

The Little Match Girl
ISBN 0 7496 6576 9*
ISBN 0 7496 6582 3

The Little Mermaid
ISBN 0 7496 6577 7*
ISBN 0 7496 6583 1

The Little Red Hen
ISBN 0 7496 6578 5*
ISBN 0 7496 6585 8

The Nightingale
ISBN 0 7496 6579 3*
ISBN 0 7496 6586 6

Thumbelina
ISBN 0 7496 6580 7*
ISBN 0 7496 6587 4

RHYME TIME
Squeaky Clean
ISBN 0 7496 6805 9

Craig's Crocodile
ISBN 0 7496 6806 7

Felicity Floss: Tooth Fairy
ISBN 0 7496 6807 5

Captain Cool
ISBN 0 7496 6808 3

Monster Cake
ISBN 0 7496 6809 1

The Super Trolley Ride
ISBN 0 7496 6810 5

The Royal Jumble Sale
ISBN 0 7496 6594 7*
ISBN 0 7496 6811 3

But, Mum!
ISBN 0 7496 6595 5*
ISBN 0 7496 6812 1

Dan's Gran's Goat
ISBN 0 7496 6596 3*
ISBN 0 7496 6814 8

Lighthouse Mouse
ISBN 0 7496 6597 1*
ISBN 0 7496 6815 6

Big Bad Bart
ISBN 0 7496 6599 8*
ISBN 0 7496 6816 4

Ron's Race
ISBN 0 7496 6600 5*
ISBN 0 7496 6817 2

* hardback